# A Promise Fulfilled

To Donna,

Randall Carpenter

*Randall L Carpenter*

*Oct 2021*

PAGE PUBLISHING, INC.
New York, NY

First originally published by Page Publishing, Inc. 2017

ISBN 978-1-64027-994-0 (Paperback)
ISBN 978-1-64027-995-7 (Digital)

Printed in the United States of America

This book is dedicated to all my friends on Facebook who have faithfully followed me, given me inspiration, and continually motivated me to write for them each day. Thank you for your love and friendship. This book would have been impossible without you and God's loving mercy.

# CONTENTS

# FOREWORD

In October of 2011, I was the picture of health, a certified personal Trainer with fifty former clients and a workout phenom. Unfortunately, on the inside I had two coronary blockages and a diseased aortic valve. During a workout, I passed out and soon had open-heart surgery to do two bypasses and replace my diseased aortic valve with an artificial aortic valve. My physical life dramatically changed overnight. While in the hospital recovering, I realized God had saved my life for a reason, and I asked Him to show me what that was. It wasn't long before thoughts of sharing His love and a little wisdom with others through a daily inspirational was His answer. This book is the fulfillment of a promise I made to God for saving my life. He gave me a purpose, and every day I feel led by God to write about His love and a little wisdom that he has blessed me with. I write because I love all of you, but I also write because God first loved me. His faith, hope, and love guide me every day, and I will never stop telling others about Him.

# INTRODUCTION

Living a Christian life is not always an easy thing to do. There are so many forces working to destroy the belief in God. There seems to be a constant drive to remove any reference to God or faith or any belief in a life after this. What baffles me is why someone would not want to believe in God and a wonderful afterlife once we are gone? What do you have to lose by believing? If there is an afterlife and you are wrong, then you have made the biggest mistake of your life and your eternity. I'm sure there are many reasons people could give for not believing, but why take the chance? Also, the love of God is unconditional, pure, and free. It is built on forgiveness and understanding. Like this book, it is about faith, hope, and love. How could you not want to be a part of that? Of course, many people are quick to dismiss something if they don't understand it, can't live up to it, or if it makes them uncomfortable to believe in something they cannot see. Not believing in something you cannot see is ridiculous. You cannot see luck, but people believe in it. You cannot see oxygen, but you know it is there because without it you would die. As a Christian, we want to love people into a relationship with Jesus Christ, so they can be happy and secure. We can do this best not by the words we speak, but by the love and hope with share with others.

This book is about the love of Jesus Christ and finding the faith, hope, and love in your life. We all have days when we feel all alone. With God in your life, you are never alone. He is always there to talk to, and He is always there with loving arms to embrace you. I hope you find within the words of this book peace, love, assurance, and inspiration. I hope my words touch your heart and let you know that someone cared enough to reach out to you. How we love one another and the hope we project to each other is what helps all of us get through this life. I hope my words of faith, hope, and love give you purpose and enrich your life.

** In some devotionals, you will read lessons also taught in other ones. Some lessons bear repeating.

# FAITH

# The Meaning of Faith

*"Now faith is the assurance of things hoped for, the conviction of things not seen. Indeed, by faith our ancestors received approval. By faith we understand that the worlds were prepared by the words of God, so that what is seen was made from things that are not visible."*

*—Hebrews 11: 1–3 NRSV*

*Sometimes, we feel our hardships outnumber our blessings. That's because most blessings exist quietly, but hardships demand our attention.*

Life is a collection of blessings and hardships that come into our life at different times. One quietly lives in our life and rarely demands we notice it, and the other screams loudly for our attention. Because we are loved by God, we receive blessings without realizing it. We are granted life, health, and forgiveness. We are blessed with beauty all around us and an ability to enjoy it through our emotions. But not all our life will be one blessing after another. There will be hardships that arrive. Those hardships will scream loudly for our attention. They will overshadow our every blessing so greatly, we will begin to think God has abandoned us. This will never happen. Though the hardships may overwhelm us, God's love always surrounds us. He is there to give you comfort and strength. It's hard to see your blessings when you are dealing with a hardship. That's OK. Do what you have to do to deal with the hardship, but never forget that you have someone to talk to who loves you. He is always ready to listen when you are ready to talk.

*When you pray and can't find the right words to say, don't worry, God knows your heart, and the words you search for are written there.*

Praying is essential to our Christian life. Without prayer, we feel lost in our walk through life. The problem we all encounter when praying is our mind begins to wander and the words we meant to say leave us. This happens more often when we pray out loud and in front of others. Don't be concerned with what you say because God already knew the prayer you needed before you tried to say it. Our every problem, desire, and need is written in our heart, and God reads our heart every day.

*In life, we cannot help but be sad at times. This is why we must always have a blessing in our pocket that we can take out to lift us up.*

We have so many things to be thankful for that we should never run out of ones to keep in our pocket. As I wrote a few days ago, blessings arrive quietly in our life and problems seem to yell for our attention. Sad times are going to happen. There are going to be disappointments and heartbreaks that happen to us. We must be prepared for them and when they happen, we have a good memory or a realized blessing to help us through. No sadness will ever be too difficult that your heart can't overcome it. Some may never leave your mind, but your heart will begin to fill your sadness with a realization of how blessed you once were. These blessings will help you accept what you will never forget and lift you up.

*It's not the everyday problems that test our faith. It's the sudden and unexpected moments where we see nothing but pain within them.*

*Faith* is a word made up of many parts. It is our strength when we need it, our foundation when we make a stand upon it, and our reason for how we act, how we think, and how we treat others. As a Christian, our faith is our life. But even the strongest faith can be tested by life events and tragedies in the world. We see and hear about disasters that claim many lives. We read about children being molested and abused. And we learn about someone dying suddenly in a car wreck or killed by a drunk driver. These senseless events cut deeply into our heart, and we ask why did this have to happen? For a moment we wonder why God would allow this, and in our grief we even think God caused it. These are the times we are most tested. God does not causes tragedies in our life or in the world. He does not decide one day to take someone we love away from us. God is love and He hurts as much as we do when these tragedies happen. There are many reasons why bad things happen, and none of them include the hand of God. We must gain our strength through God that He loves us, and we can go to Him for comfort. Don't let the events of this world test your faith. Your faith should always be your comfort, and it should not waver at any time.

*We're touched by an angel every day. The stranger who spoke and smiled and the person you just couldn't stop looking at ... both were angels.*

Throughout our life, we have angels that lead us where we need to go, dissuade us from going to places we don't belong, and save us from moments in our life where we can't understand how we avoided serious injury. We encounter people who change our life. We hear or read words that answer questions we have always had. And we see someone we feel drawn to for no apparent reason. These are the angels in our life whispering to us. Those moments when you suddenly feel a soft breeze and have no idea where it came from, that is when an angel has passed by you. Angels in our life are not people who possess great powers, but people in our life that possess great influence. People are put in our path for a reason, and that reason is always for our benefit. Listen for the whispers, watch for the moments of love, and smile at everyone ... you never know if they may be your angel today.

*When life becomes too much, cross your arms and put a hand on top of each shoulder. Now look down. The cross it makes may be sideways, but it's right over your heart. God is always that close to you.*

I was sitting at my computer last night working on what to write you this morning. I had written three or four different ones and each didn't seem right to me. After about 30 minutes of writing, deleting, re-writing and eventually discarding several attempts, I stopped and rested my elbows on the table in front of my computer. Due to the height of the table, I could not cross my arms and my hands rested on the top of my shoulders. As if to start praying for some guidance, I looked down and saw my arms had formed a sideways cross. That's all it took. People ask me all the time where I get my inspiration. Well, you now know my secret. I blindly stumble across it. Have a blessed day.

*Sometimes in life, you have to step without knowing where your foot will land. Most decisions can be thought out, but some must be by faith.*

Leaps of faith are never easy. Without faith we become like stone paralyzed by our own fears. Making some decisions in life can be difficult. We are often pulled in two directions and can't decide which one is more important. The older we get the harder decision are to make. When we're younger, we lack the years of experience that make us sometimes over think what we need to do. Being innocently ignorant has its advantages sometimes. Knowing where to place your next footprint can worry us unless we develop confidence in ourselves. Most decisions are not permanent. Some cannot be reversed, but most can be rethought after we make them. Actually, making decisions is easy…making the right ones is the hard part.

*Sometimes, the greatest things in our life are the things we take for granted. Assume nothing is forever and everything is a blessing from God.*

Many times in life we say we are blessed that something happened. It is usually something out of the ordinary that didn't normally happen. We notice it and feel we are so fortunate. Being grateful for special things that happen is normal, but these kind of things happen to us all the time, and we don't realize it. We take our greatest blessings in life for granted. Being alive and able to appreciate all the beauty and wonder around us is a special blessing. Feeling the love of someone and having someone to love is a special blessing. We all see, hear, touch, and feel blessings every day that we take for granted. Maybe we should slow down and look around occasionally and realize how blessed we are in so many ways. I feel blessed to have you reading this and everything I write. Thank you for being one of my blessings, and I promise I will never take you for granted.

*Living a faithful life isn't meant to be in the shadow of a steeple, but in the bright lights of a world that casts a shadow for all to see.*

Living a life of faith is never easy. On Sundays, in the shadow of the steeple, it is easy to feel you are doing your part to show everyone you are a Christian. The difficult part is doing so every day when the lights of the world are on you and everyone can see the way you live your life. Living a faithful life requires commitment, sacrifices, and a resolve that may set you apart from others. It requires that you lead more than you follow. Faith is believing something you cannot see. Living a faithful life is knowing what you believe and letting others see it in you. It takes strength, but no more than God gives us every day.

*A life without God is like driving with your eyes closed. You may do well on the straight a-ways, but the curves are going to get you.*

God in my life has always been something that gave me direction, strength, and resolve. Having God in my life has gotten me through my worst tragedies and made my triumphs sweeter because I could thank him for his blessings. Life is not a straight road that we blindly travel on autopilot. There are many sharp curves we approach where we can't see what's around the bend. This is when we rely on our faith in God to get us around the curve. The blessings we receive every day give us hope, and with hope in your life...you can accomplish anything.

*The hand you extend to help someone
is not your own. It's the hand of God
that once was extended to you and
is now extended through you.*

The strength of your faith determines the belief in your heart about how much God blesses you in your life. What you believe and the abilities of God to extend to you a hand of hope and love determines the strength of your faith. We are meant to be the ones that spread God's love. When we live our faith and we extend a hand of help, then we are extending to someone God's hand through us. We cannot fix every problem that is presented to us, but we can do what we can. Extending a hand of help may be done in many ways. It may be financial help. It may be word of encouragement or empathy. And it may be lifting someone from their despair by physically helping them. God never limits us to any form of love that we want to display. God is love, and if we do for others through a heart of love, we cannot go wrong. Blessings come in many forms. What we receive, we are to give back a portion of to expand God's kingdom. Never doubt the love of God and what God can do. God places no limitation on us, and we should place no limitations on Him.

*When you love God, your prayers are heard sooner because they only have to travel as far as your heart for God to hear them.*

Loving the one God and treating others like you want to be treated were two very important lessons of Jesus's teachings (Luke 10:27). Trying to live a Christian life is very difficult unless you follow this scripture. When you try to worship more than one God, it becomes impossible to worship the one God. We are instructed to love God with all our heart and all our mind. We are told to put away false idols and let our love for God be our guide through life. We some-times allow other things in our life to control us, and we try to justify it by saying, "There are things I have to do to be accepted or to live the life I want to live." It's OK to seek a lifestyle that will please you, but we are supposed to create our lifestyle around Christ's teach-ings ... not Christ's teachings around our lifestyle.

When you have God in your heart, and your heart is filled with the joy of knowing you are loved, it makes praying so much more meaningful. When you live closer to God's teachings, you feel more secure, and that is what we all seek in life. God does not expect us to live a life of total piety. He realizes we must fit into this world. But it is possible to make the life you live fit into the teachings of Jesus Christ. You are loved by God in every way. No matter what you do, have done, or will do could change that in any way. As a thank you for such love, all God asks is you try to follow His teachings. When you sincerely try, it could change your life forever.

*Putting things in God's hands is hard.*
*We want to control what happens*
*and feel we are doing everything we*
*can. In God's hands is everything.*

This is one of the toughest things for any Christian to do. Partly because we don't really understand what that means, and partly because we have a hard time relinquishing control. Our life is indeed controlled by many things we have no control over. Some we create for ourselves, and others are just life. Our desire to succeed, in spite of these barriers, is our strength of character as well as our strength of determination. There are no paths in life that are all downhill … sometimes the quest to overcome what we cannot control requires a lot of effort. Placing our trust in something we cannot control is overwhelming and makes no sense. When we place things in God's hands, it is not relinquishing control, but asking for direction. We are not meant to just sit down and wait for Him to fix everything. When we place things in God's hands, we are actually asking Him to help us do what WE need to do to fix our problem. It is not a matter of God doing it *for* us, but God doing it *through* us. We must still make the efforts to fix our problem. Placing it in God's hands means asking for guidance, not action. It means believing God will hold on to the *worry* part of fixing the problem while we work on the solution to the problem. Placing it in God's hands is really asking Him to place His hands around yours and guiding your efforts toward a solution to your problem.

# *Within you there's a strength that is stronger than your doubts, greater than your expectations, and answers every question. It's called faith.*

Within everyone there is strength that they do not know exists. Everyone has this strength, but only those who draw from its source realize why they have the strength. Some people think this strength comes from their own resolve and, therefore, is centered in them. This strength is called *faith*. Some people think *faith* is the belief in something that you cannot see. This is not entirely true. If you have true faith, you see all around you the proof of why you believe. You feel in your heart the reason why you believe. Faith is believing something will happen because of your understanding it exists to guide you. Faith is stronger than your greatest weakness if your faith is more a part of you than your weaknesses. Making yourself vulnerable to your faith and not to your weakness is the key. You use your faith to overcome any obstacle, stop you from doing things you know are wrong and, most importantly, your faith is there to give you a reason to not be manipulated by the devil. Temptation is one of our greatest weaknesses. Temptation is that voice you hear that tells you to forget all you heard, all you have seen, all you have learned, and all you stand for. Temptation is more than giving into something. It's more than committing a sin. It's also compromise. Use your faith to avoid temptation, and you will find a strength you never knew you possessed. Make your life about your faith in God and His teaching. If you let your faith lead you, you will no longer have to fear your weaknesses. Your faith will be your answer to every question.

## *Displaying your faith in church is easy. Some find it difficult to do so outside the church. God's church has no walls. Live your faith.*

Those of us who go to church enjoy our time there and feel fulfilled and uplifted by the experience. There is something wonderful about spending time with God in a place where everyone is there for the same purpose. This is called a community of faith. We rely on this community of faith to be the place we feel safest and most comfortable worshiping God. But once we leave the safety and comfort of the church, some of us no longer feel that comfort level. We all have a tendency to rise to a level of our own self-proclaimed incompetence, and we lose our confidence in what to say. Is this because we really don't have faith, we only have friends we want to see every Sunday? Is it because we are scared to mention our faith outside the confines of the church walls? Maybe this is true to a point, but until we realize the church has no walls, we will always feel this discomfort. Sadly, our society has mandated that we cannot discuss our religion in some contexts. I suppose that is OK if we don't want to be approached by people of other religious faiths. What we must realize is our faith is not something we display a couple of times a week. It is something we display every day. Your greatest display of your faith and beliefs is seen by others every time you act or react to something. The way you act and talk and treat others are what people notice most. If your behavior does not mirror the belief in your heart, then people wonder if what they see every day is really what you profess to be. Christ never had to remind people what he was about; they saw it in his actions and reactions. There are no walls in Christ's church. If you feel uncomfortable for any reason talking about your faith, then let your behavior be your testimony. It has always been true...actions speak louder than words.

# *What we take for granted every day are actually miracles that have already happened in our life. Your ability to read this is one of them.*

The blessings we receive from God are countless. The miracles that happen around us every day, we often overlook. Sometimes, the greatest things in our life are the things we take for granted. Assume nothing is forever and everything is a blessing from God. The seasons we enjoy and the changing of the trees from barren branches to leaf-filled wonder is a miracle. The tides moving in and out all caused by the gravitational forces of the sun and moon on the oceans of the earth is amazing. And, of course, the greatest miracle God ever created, the conception of a child from a single egg that is fertilized and starts to grow into the beautiful baby we one day hold and love. We need to see the miracles around us and realize how much God loves us as He continues to give us what we need every day. It is not important that we know every miracle God gives us, but it is important that we take the time to see and appreciate the miracles He produces for us every day. Realizing our blessings can be better achieved by having an active prayer life. If you pray daily, you will hear in your prayer the miracles you know are important to you. We all have different wants and needs, and God knows this. God knows our heart and knows our needs. He loves us more than mere words can explain. Find your miracles in life and rejoice in them. God has a plan for you.

*Sometimes, we can feel so alone all we hear is our own heartbeat. It's not our heartbeat we hear. It's God knocking, asking if He can come in.*

There are times in our life when we need a moment of peace. It's not to get away from anything or that we're unhappy; it's our moment for reflection. But there are also times when our heart is heavy, and we feel lost. One of the loneliest times in anyone's life will be after they have had their heart broken. A broken heart can change your life if it is accompanied by depression. In times like these, when the darkness of the night surrounds us, and the weariness of our mind brings memories of times gone by, we can hear our heart beating. The pounding in our chest takes our mind off our feeling of loss, and we begin to count the heartbeats. We listen intently to the beat of our heart and soon realize it never changes. It begins to mesmerize us, and we hear a rhythm like the tapping on a door. Slowly we relax and listen, and the tapping begins to calm us. We begin feeling relaxed, and our mind seems to see answers to what we were worrying about. We have begun to heal, and thoughts of the future enter our mind. God heard your cry and felt your pain. The sound you heard was not your heartbeat; it was God knocking at the door of your heart. Your heart responded by opening the door, and that is when you relaxed; your mind cleared and new thoughts of a future entered your life. God knows when we hurt. He feels what we feel. Don't be scared any longer. You are in the arms of God.

*What surrounds us every day are opportunities to give, to share, to help, and to understand. When we seize these opportunities, we worship God.*

Every day, we are given opportunities to live our faith. We are given chances to worship God by doing for others as we are taught in the Bible. However, we may know it's the right thing to do, but we hesitate to do it out of fear. We all have fear we live with. Some fears we harbor within us are from experience, and others, society has ingrained in us. When we seize opportunities to give to someone, to share what we have, to help without a reason and, most importantly, to show we want to understand, we worship God through our obedience. We have all seen the person on the side of the road with a sign asking for help. Our first response is to not make eye contact. Our next response is often judgment of the person and their actual need. Lastly, we begin to struggle with our emotions of what to do. We look into the rearview mirror and see if someone is behind us. We see no one, and now our emotion of wanting to help the person is embattled with our feelings of judgment, need, and a rationale for driving past them. Before we can settle this in our mind, we are past the person, and the battle stops. We tell ourselves it's OK because we thought about doing it, and that means we are a decent person. Actually, thoughts are only part of our Christian life. What we do and don't do is the testimony of our life. Our actions speak louder than our thoughts. Opportunities missed to show your Christian teachings are opportunities lost. What we refuse to do for others begins to add up and becomes our mantra. Don't let the world tell you how you should respond to opportunities to serve God through actions. You are God's hands, feet, eyes, and voice. Don't ever forget that.

*God knew what He was doing when He created us. It takes more muscles to frown than to smile ... maybe He intended for us to smile more than frown.*

The way in which we think about ourselves and the life we have is essential to our happiness. Our self-esteem and attitude toward others is what gives us the strength and desire we need to make the best of everything in life. The best way I have heard someone explain how to approach life is the following: "Have an attitude of gratitude." Having an "attitude of gratitude" means you appreciate what you have and what you have been blessed with. Sometimes people don't realize what they have, and when you bring it to their attention, they deny having a bad attitude. This is called "having an attitude about your attitude." If someone tells you that you have a bad attitude, maybe you should act and not react to that observation. What we convey to others in life may not be what we intend to convey. Therefore, if someone mentions your demeanor, you may need to listen. When God made us, it's obvious He intended that we smile more than frown. This is obvious because when He constructed our face, He put in more muscles to make a frown than a smile. It requires more effort on our part to frown than smile. Why not take the route of least resistance and smile more and frown less? One of my father's favorite quotes was "For every person who sees you and knows you, there are hundreds who see you and don't know you. The only impression they have of you is what they see at that moment. Always look your best, act your best, and treat people with respect. You never know who's watching ... it could be a child." This being absolutely true, don't you think a smile seen by others will make a better impression than a frown?

*No one knows the silent tears we shed every day from a pain so deep, we lose sight of our self. Thankfully, God never loses sight of us.*

Tears that fall from our eyes can be seen. Tears of pain that fall from our heart are often hidden. We never know who is hurting inside. Part of being alive is suffering pain. Christ suffered different types of pain throughout His life right up to the moment He was crucified and endured unimaginable pain. Pain is the physical and mental release of something that is wrong with our body or our emotional state. When something is physically hurting us, we suffer. We seek painkillers that will take it away or mask it for a period of time. Hopefully, over time the pain goes away or lessened to a point we can endure it. But pain that hurts us emotionally is far less treatable. This is true for a number of reasons. If we are physically hurting, we will not hesitate to seek a remedy for that pain. If we are emotionally hurting, we will try to fix ourselves or learn to live with the pain. We will try to hide our pain or blame ourselves for the pain. Being hurt emotionally never shows on us physically unless we wear the hurt by the way we act. Sadly, the reason for the chronic pain often lies within us. We had our feelings hurt by someone we loved and/ or trusted and, we are holding a grudge. We cannot forgive ourselves for something we did recently or in our past. Or we feel lost because of our situation in life, and loneliness begins to creep in. The loneliness we feel is not always caused by the absence of people in our life. It's also a loss of love we have for ourselves. No one knows the silent tears we shed every day from a pain so deep, we lose sight of our self. Thankfully, God never loses sight of us. If you are feeling a pain that is causing you to not enjoy life, seek help. God gave us emotions so we could love life, not have to endure it. The sun will not shine brightly every day, but it still comes up every day. Look for the sunbeams in your life. They are there. They may be behind a cloud that you need to brush out of the way. Forgive yourself for anything you feel guilty about because God has already forgiven you. You are loved. Remember this: "There is nothing you have every done or will every do that will make God love you any more or any less than He does right now." His love is unconditional and free. Embrace it and let it help you heal.

*There are two benefits to praying before a decision. The first is placing your trust in God. The other is it makes you think before you act.*

Everyone prays in one way or another. Even those who say they are nonreligious pray every day. They may not bow their head or fold their hands, but they either say the prayer to themselves or out loud. This is true because everyone has said this in their life, "I wish…" or "I hope…" If they are not praying, who are they talking to?

Prayer is essential in leading a Christian life. As those who follow Christ's teachings know, being able to slow your life down and feel you are communicating with someone who never judges you, never ignores you, and loves you unconditionally is amazing. Prayer in your life makes a difference in you. When you pray to God, you are accomplishing two very critical parts of making good decisions. The first is trusting God enough to go to Him with your questions. The second, and this is very important in making good decisions, is you have an opportunity to hear if you really know what you are asking. When you pray sincerely, you explain to God what you need, want, or desire. By doing so, you have a chance to find out if you really know what you are praying about. By explaining it to God, you hear yourself saying what you need to hear. The more you pray about something, the more you realize if you're making a right decision. There is nothing wrong with taking the time to pray about something. People may push you to make a quick decision on something, but it is a rare occasion when a decision must be made immediately. I worked in retail for years. There is no such thing as "this is the last day" or "the price goes up tomorrow." The company is in business to sell whatever you're looking at. If they are willing to sell it for a certain price today, they will sell it for that price tomorrow. If not, then you are no less or better off than you were the day before. Always pray before you act. It will make your decisions easier to accept. There is never a better time to pray than the moment you realize you haven't. There is no step that leads you closer to God than the last step you take before bending your knees to pray. God is always ready to listen.

*There is the belief that we're only held accountable for what we say and not what we think. So does that mean that God only listens when we pray out loud? I think not.*

What we say and what we think are often two different things. We can think anything we want, but as long as we don't say it out loud, no one hears it and, therefore, no one can hold it against us. That may be true when it comes to offending others or being held accountable by others, but not when it comes to pleasing God. If this were true, only our prayers spoken out loud would be heard by God. This, of course, is not true. God hears us however we pray. If this were not true, why do we feel accountable to God for what we think? We are supposed to be pure of heart and mind. What we think in our mind is just as clear to God as what we speak out loud to others. Being pure of heart means not harboring grudges, judgments, or deceitful thoughts. When we speak unkindly or think unkindly about someone, we have wronged them just as if we had publicly berated them. I know it is difficult to be pure of thought. Our emotions get the best of us and we find it necessary to strike out at others. Before you say something that you might regret one day, you need to think before you speak. The best way to do so is to answer as many questions with *yes* or *no* as possible. The questions you cannot answer with yes or no need to be preceded with a pause to allow you to think before you answer. By doing so, you will not answer a question or respond to anything with an emotionally driven answer. Lastly, before you respond to something that has upset you, ask yourself if you really need to say something, or can you ignore it. You have to realize, not everything that upsets us has to be responded to.

*A heart shattered by tragedy seems*
*broken beyond repair until God*
*begins to mend it with memories.*
*Slowly, it starts to beat again.*

All too often, we hear about something tragic that happened. Drug overdoses, drunk driving, or domestic abuse that destroys an entire family. Why does this happen? It's the grip of addiction. People never consider themselves as addicted as others are. If we cannot learn from our own mistakes, we must learn to do so from the mistakes of others. Sometimes, our greatest tragedies in life are not the things that happen to others, but the things that happen to others that we don't allow to change us. Sadly, sometimes those who are addicted cannot do this for themselves. This is why people who love them must do this for them. We cannot be afraid to confront those who are on the path to destruction. It may save their life or the lives of innocent people all around them.

Life is a journey, and along that journey our paths cross with others on their own journey. The friendships that form create happiness in our life. That happiness becomes a part of us and gives us strength and joy. When that bond is broken suddenly, we don't know what to do or feel. The loss goes beyond the physical absence of our friend. It pierces our heart like nothing we have ever felt before. But like every tragedy in life, there are no words that can be said that can begin to heal our grief. This is when we must rely on our faith and other friends to help us begin to heal. When you have a shattered heart, it seems like it will never beat correctly again. God loves us, and when He knows we are ready, He begins placing memories in our heart to heal the cracks.

*Developing an attitude of grace is remembering to open your heart when you open your eyes. Life is not what you see, but how you see it.*

Your attitude is part of everything you do. It's part of your interaction with others. It's part of how you do your job. And it's the one thing people will notice about you after your appearance. Your attitude can make you even more appealing to others. Since your reputation is not what you think of yourself, but what others think of you, having a good attitude is essential. We all go through mood swings and have things that bother us, but being able to maintain a good attitude in the face of ongoing annoyances is necessary. People who have a good attitude have more people that confide in them. If you have a poor attitude and complain about things, people will listen to you for a short period of time and then begin to ignore you or avoid you. It is difficult to be effective with others if people hate being around you. God gave us emotions to love our life, not to take it out on others. You must be consistent in your behavior, pleasant in your communications, and understanding with others when mistakes are made. If you are, people will try harder not to make mistakes, and when they do, they will be more receptive to your comments about how to do better next time.

## *The blessings in our life are never hidden. The key is to realize how blessed you are before it becomes how blessed you were.*

We have many blessings in our life. God loves us, and because of this, He blesses us in so many ways. The beauty that surrounds us is there for our enjoyment. The emotions He places within us allows us to laugh, to cry, and to embrace all that makes our life worth living. None of our blessings from God are hidden. They are there for us to see if we take the time to look for them. One of the greatest blessings in our life are those we love. These are the people who have loved us, nurtured us, and gotten us through times in our life. They are also friends who have become more like brothers and sisters than friends. Having these people in our life is a blessing, and we must realize this. The important part about your blessings is realizing that they are not permanent and can be gone today in a heartbeat. Taking the time to look where you are blessed is saying you realize how blessed you are. Take nothing for granted in your life because blessings are a fragile thing that have a lifespan. They live as long as you recognize them and appreciate their existence. If you do this, then the blessings will continue to live in your memories. The key is to realize how blessed you are, before you have to say to yourself how blessed you were.

*As long as you believe in you ... you
will never fail. Failure is what others
think of someone, not what someone
should think of themselves.*

One of our greatest fears in life is the fear of failure. We fear it so much, we will avoid doing something we want to do because of it. Fear of failure has stifled many great thoughts and stopped many people from accomplishing what they could have, had they only tried. The important thing you must remember is that God never made anyone who was not successful. When you opened your eyes at birth, you began a series of successes that have never ended.

The term *failure* is an interesting word. What is failure? What constitutes failure? Is it because you did not do what you felt you could or should do? Or is it what someone else defines as a failure? We all have varying abilities. My ability to do something has nothing to do with your ability to do something. Just because I can do it and you cannot does not make you a failure. My father, W. Howard Carpenter once told me everyone is ignorant ... just on different subjects. The same would go for failure then. Everyone is a failure, just on different things attempted. Of course, this is not at all true, but when people refer to someone as a failure, they are basing it on their own opinion, and there is no basis for it. Where one person succeeds and another cannot does not constitute failure because no two people are the same, and no two situations are the same. Failure should never be something someone thinks of themselves. If you believe in you and you make your best attempt at whatever, then you have succeeded. The mere attempt to do something is a success. Sometimes in life we are afraid to take a step due to uncertainty. Nothing in life was ever accomplished without some degree of uncertainty. You cannot succeed if you do not try. But not trying doesn't make you a failure ... It just makes you wish you had at least made an attempt.

*Strength of character is when you realize your mistakes, ignore the judgments of others, and find within yourself a strength you never knew.*

If there is one thing that separates one person from another, it has to be strength of character. People with character look at life differently than those who do not possess character. They deal with their losses, as well as their triumphs differently. A person of character accepts their mistakes and does not try to blame others. A person of character never passes judgment on others. Being judgmental is the first sign of low self-esteem. Judging others is easier than trying to get to know them and realizing you're wrong in your judgment. Character is developed over time by following the positive examples in your life and by following the examples Jesus gave to us. Having strength of character is something your faith gives you. You know the strength within your faith is greater than the weaknesses in your life. Whatever your mind lacks in resistance, your faith can overcome. Relying on your faith to lead you and help you make good decisions is showing strength of character. You are the person you choose to be. You set standards for yourself, and you live by them every day without compromise, discussion, or reservation. You must remember, if you do not have principles you live by, you will always be open to someone's manipulation. Be strong and know that you are loved by God.

## *Our Christian life is not created each Sunday. It's created between Sundays by the way we live our life and apply God's teachings.*

Living a Christian life is not easy. We can hope for a life of easy decisions that perfectly mirrors our faith, but that is not going to happen. We try to follow the path that Jesus followed, but it almost seems impossible. We have to work at it and try not to let temptation get the best of us. Temptation is one of the hardest things to avoid. It surrounds us and never lets up on us. Temptation is that voice your hear that tells you to forget all you have heard, all you have seen, all you have learned, and all you stand for. Fortunately, when we go to church on Sunday the temptation we feel seems to go away. We are caught up in the spirit and the community of faith that frees us from what we endured through the week.

Well, Sunday is over and Monday is here. Time to see what you remember from the sermon and how you can live the life you want to live. The best way to try to live a Christian life is to live your life as if you were writing a book for a child to read. If you follow your faith, your book will contain more illustrations than words. This is not supposed to make you paranoid, but it will make you think about what you say and do. It will make you think about where you go and the decisions you make daily. You want to make your life a reflection of what you want to see in others. When you lead by example, your life speaks louder than any words you may say. Our Christian life is not created on Sunday, it's created between each Sunday by the way we live our life and apply God's teachings.

*Overcoming mistakes in your life is more a matter of letting go of what you are and realizing who you are in God's eyes.*

Making mistakes is part of being human. There is no one alive who has not made a mistake in their life. Some mistakes are worse than others, but allowing your mistakes to control your life is never good. Not everything is going to go right every day. When it doesn't, you have two choices. You can act and fix it or react and complain about it. Wearing your mistakes like a yoke around your neck will accomplish nothing. Our greatest challenges in life have always been our greatest teacher. What we learn in adversity, we never forget. Making mistakes has always been one of everyone's biggest worries. No one likes making mistakes, but making a mistake is not a life sentence of distrust by those around you or a reason to think less of yourself. If those around you care about you, they will remember when they made mistakes and treat you like they wanted to be treated after they made a mistake. God understands that we are not perfect. But in His eyes you were created perfectly, and you have remained perfect in His eyes. You must remember, there is nothing you could ever do or anything you have ever done that would make God love you any more or any less than He does right at this moment. God's love for you is unconditional and consistent. Lean on it and rely on it because it will heal your heart and your life.

*We often fall short of our own expectations but never those of God's. He loves us as we are, as we will be or completely broken.*

Years ago I wrote the following to a friend of mine, and it has been something I have quoted many times over the years: "We all have a tendency to rise to a level of our own self-proclaimed incompetence and, therefore, lose our confidence in what to say or do." I know I have done this many times. I have approached things in my life that I wanted to do and wondered at what point I would lose my confidence. At one time in my life, the only thing I felt any confidence in doing was writing. But because of my deeply felt incompetence in other areas, I never let anyone know I wrote. It hindered my success dramatically. But I was able to overcome this phobia when I became closer to God. God loves us, and He has high expectations for us, but loves us no matter what we obtain or don't obtain in life. He is the ultimate wonderful Father that loves us not matter what and is there for us in all situations. Let me repeat something I have already written in this book, but bears repeating. You must remember…there is nothing you could ever do or anything you have ever done that would make God love you any more or any less than He does right at this moment.

Live your life with the fullest intentions of succeeding and making everyone around you proud. But if circumstances overtake you, or your weaknesses are greater than your strengths and you fall down in life, do not fear. God is there to help you up and hold you up. God will not do it for you, He will do it through you. Once you have found your purpose from God, the strength within your faith will be greater than the weaknesses in your life. Whatever your mind lacks in resistance, your faith will overcome. God bless.

*Miracles don't happen at a distance ... they happen right in front of us. Look for them and cherish the love within each.*

Life is a collection of miracles that happen every day, and we only occasionally notice and rarely give thanks for it. Recognizing the miracles in our life usually doesn't happen until a tragedy occurs or someone close to us is dramatically and unexpectedly cured or saved. These are the noticeable miracles, but not the greatest ones in our life. Our greatest miracle happens when we open our eyes in the morning, and we have been given another day to love all that God provides for us. Miracles do not need to be thunder-and-lightning moments. They can be soft whispers or barely noticeable events that seem to line up perfectly. Our lives are made up of moments of brilliance punctuated by periods of normalcy. If it wasn't for our miracles from God, we would never get from place to place alive.

Do not take for granted the love of God. The beauty that He surrounds you with and the ability to enjoy it are all miracles. What we see, hear, smell, and touch are all miracles God has given us. Learn to embrace the miracles that surround you. Learn love, what is there to love, and never take for granted anything. We are freely given miracles from God, and we should say *thank you* every day.

*The blessings God gives us aren't meant for just us. They are meant to also bless others. When you share your blessings ... you honor God.*

Every day, God blesses our life. He gives us the sunshine in the morning, the sunset in the evening, and the ability to enjoy everything in between. More importantly, He gives us love, compassion, and empathy. He gives us eyes to see, ears to hear, and a voice to express our happiness. When we realize our blessings and we share them with others, we thank God for them. I know seeing your blessings among the struggles of life may be hard, but they are there. You are loved by God. He wants you to be happy. It only takes one smile to open the eyes of your heart to all the blessings God gives you.

The blessings God gives us, we choose to either use them, save them, or ignore them. The blessings He gives us are meant for us to improve our closer walk with Him and for us to bless others. The money we make, the health we enjoy, and the physical strength we are blessed with are meant to be shared. When we do this, we are honoring God and thanking Him for giving us these blessings. Sharing the blessings we receive has always been something Christ's teachings has taught us. We are meant to lead others by our gifts and change others through our example. The blessings we share are the blessings we recognize and were meant for others, as well as us. What we give will surely reap rewards for God's kingdom. Jesus gave of himself at every opportunity. He provided for others as He testified of His faith in His father. It has been said that giving is better than receiving. But from a Christian standpoint, we are not giving ... we are only sharing what we have already received.

RANDALL CARPENTER

*Sometimes, the key to hearing God's voice isn't listening, but feeling. He whispers to our heart and suddenly we feel more certain what to do.*

God speaks to us in everything around us. The beauty of the seasons, the peacefulness of the rain, and the majesty of a sunset and sunrise. But sometimes we are unsure of what to do because of all the things in our life we try to consider before making a decision. These are the things that bounce around in our head and keep us from making decisions. God doesn't try to compete with those things, He just quietly whispers to our heart what we need to do, and suddenly we are more certain of ourselves. When we follow our heart, we are recognizing God's voice. If we have prayed and asked God to guide us, then following our heart is not difficult. He speaks to us quietly, and sometimes He speaks to us boldly. When we fail to hear what He is saying, He sometimes has to nudge us. Your heart is God's closest means of talking to you. There is always that little voice in your head, but it sometimes gets drowned out by all the ways your mind can rationalize any behavior or decision. Follow you heart and you will be following God. You must remember, sometimes your heart will tell you not to do something, and you won't believe it. Trust in your heart, and you will be trusting in God.

*Today may be just another day, but you could be a miracle to someone and never know it. It only takes a moment of grace to change a heart.*

There are many moments in our life when we have a chance to teach, lead, or change someone. How we project what's in our heart can make a difference not only in ourselves, but also in those around us. There are countless numbers of people searching for a path to follow, a reason to live, and a joy they can hold on to. If we project the love and compassion we possess, we can be a miracle to others. God gives us the ability to change ourselves and those around us, and that is a miracle in itself.

44

*May the Lord bless you and keep you.*
*May your day be filled with sunshine*
*and your steps lead you toward the*
*horizon of a beautiful sunset.*

The blessings of God are all around. His love for us is shown repeatedly in the beauty of nature, the ability to love one another, and in our sunrises and sunsets. We begin each day with the opening of God's eyes and the rays of sunlight slowly cresting the horizon. With light to see where we are and where we shall go, we begin to harvest what we have sown. We end each day with God slowly closing His eyes and the sun disappearing into the darkness. We are given time to rest and moments to slow our pace. With the ending of each day, we can look back at our time spent with gratitude and pride that we made a difference in God's kingdom. Never fail to thank God for what you have, and with a grateful heart praise Him in your prayers.

# When someone says, "I love you, this much," I hope their arms are spread widely because that's how Jesus said, "I loved you, this much."

Let me explain the meaning of this writing by sharing with you what I've written years ago titled "How Much He Loved Me."

I turned to the Lord one day
And I asked Him how much He loved me?
He looked at me and with arms spread widely
He said, "I love you this much, my son."
Not understanding, I asked,
"But how much is that, my Lord?"
Once again, His arms spread widely, He said,
"I love you this much, my child."
"But Lord," I said,
"Don't you know any other way of showing me?"
"I know no better way of showing you, my child,
But the way in which I am."
"How about a priceless gift?"
"Or a trip to show me how much you love me?"
Once again the Lord looked at me and said,
Gesturing as before,
"I love you this much, my son."
"I have but this single way of showing you."
Not yet grasping what my Lord was saying,
I begged for Him to tell me more.
But my Lord just looked up at me
And with arms spread widely,

As He had shown me before,
He laid down on that Cross
And showed me how much He loved me.

March 30, 1994

When we tell someone, "I love you, this much," our arms should be stretched out beside us like Jesus's arms were when He lay down on that cross and showed us how much He loved us. Be blessed because Jesus paid for your sins. All He asks is we honor Him by not denying Him to others. Your love for Him and your expressions of love are your gifts to Him for his sacrifice.

# HOPE

*"For surely I know the plans I have for you, says the Lord, plans for your welfare and not for harm, to give you a future with hope. Then when you call upon me and come and pray to me, I will hear you"*

*—Jeremiah 29: 11–12 NRSV*

*Sometimes, a single word of hope or a few notes of music can change a heart completely. Listen for your song today and let the words lead you.*

When there is a blue moment in your life, a word of hope and encouragement can make a difference. But there is something about music that touches our soul. The music, along with the words, slow us down, focus us, and hold our attention like nothing else. Music is so soothing to the soul that only a few notes of a favorite song can bring wonderful memories back in an instant. Music and the words within each one are part of us. No matter who you are, no matter what you have been through, music and the words within have touched your heart at some time in your life. The music within us is just a memory or a silent moment of reflection away. Find your song today and let it remind you that some beautiful moments never go away.

*Hope is when you know in spite of all the problems, all the noise and all the negativity ... your candle still burns brightly in the distance.*

Hope is the one thing in our life that we cannot lose. If we lose hope, we lose our ability to dream. If we cannot dream, we have no future to work toward. We are surrounded by negativity, a media that fans the problems in this country and the world, and a culture of entitlement that is causing our country to become less self-reliant and more dependent. If we maintain our hope in the face of all we are told, we will not lose sight of our future. We must lead by example and ignore all the attempted manipulation. We must have faith in our faith and follow the example that was set for us over 2,000 years ago.

*Don't let the darkness that may surround you keep you from lighting a candle of hope. It only takes a single flame to find a path to follow.*

Sadly, there is a lot of darkness that surrounds us every day. We see it, feel it, and are bombarded by it from every direction. The news media pounds away at it every day, and people begin to feel that there is no hope. Never allow anything or anyone to tell you that there is no hope in this world. The hope that exists in this world must originate in each of us. Hope is not something we should rely on someone else to give us. Hope can be a single flame flickering in the darkness that we see. When we seek hope, we seek a direction to follow. Without hope, we see no future. Without hope, we lose our desires to keep fighting. Hope can sometimes be a single step away from the darkness caused by a desire to see. Be the one holding the candle of hope for others to follow. You can be that light in the darkness if you never let go of hope.

*When hope becomes reality, it's more than the answer to a prayer. It's the display of faith that never wavered and a belief that miracles happen.*

Believing, having faith, and never losing hope are the keystones to seeing miracles happen in your life. What we never waver in believing is what becomes a reality one day. Without hope, we have no dreams. Without faith, we have no assurances, and without believing in miracles, we will never recognize our blessings. Every day that we keep hope in our heart will be another day a miracle can happen. Have a blessed day and know you are loved.

*Most roads we take aren't straight and neither is any road to success. It's not about the difficulty of our route, but the destination we seek.*

In life, we go down many roads toward something and sometimes away from something. Seeing the exact path we should take is never easy. Deciding if the path we are on is leading us toward something better is always on our mind. No path in our life is straight. There are twists, turns, bumps, hills, and valleys all along the way. I think the key is to enjoy the view from the top of the hill and not to let the time in the valley steal our dreams. No success in life is a spontaneous event ... it takes time to develop it and, sometimes, many tries.

Accomplishing anything is a struggle, no matter how easy it may have appeared at the time. In order to succeed at anything, it requires sacrifice and perseverance. Preparing yourself to succeed is vital and may determine the length of time it takes for you to succeed. The better you prepare, the faster you will do so. Preparation will prevent frustration, because frustration can cause loss of determination. If your desire to succeed is not strong enough, you will lose your focus and accept where you are right now. Every success is preceded by many unsuccessful attempts. If we got it right the first time, success would eventually mean nothing. You must keep trying until you succeed. What you do with the talent you have is not as important as what you do with the desire you possess. Great desire can overcome less talent. Apply your desire to succeed, and over time your talents will increase, and your success will arrive.

*What happened in the past is supposed to teach you what to do to assure that what happens in the future is not a repeat of past disappointments.*

I enjoyed writing this because so many of us have overcome so much in our life, and I wanted to highlight that. A lot of people admire others by what they can see someone has done. What they don't see or realize is everything that person had to overcome to accomplish what they admire. True success is not what you accomplish but what you overcome. Those are the hidden moments that lead to everything someone will do in the future.

Recognizing someone's accomplishments by the title they hold or the athletic prowess they achieve is easy. What we don't see are the obstacles they had to overcome to be in the position they are. We all face challenges in our life that make us either push harder or we allow to hold us back. Understandably, many obstacles people face are beyond their control and, therefore, impossible to overcome. But beyond these special circumstances, people who succeed have had to overcome much to be where they are. Succeeding sometimes requires ignoring the uncertainties in life and accepting the unknown as a challenge, not as a stopping point.

Being successful is not a matter of being recognized by everyone and lauded for your accomplishments. Being successful is improving your situation in life and maintaining it so others can learn from it. Wealth is not a sign of success, it's a benefit of success. Celebrity is not a sign of success, either. It is a recognition of accomplishment, but your life may still be a mess. Many people are successful just by still being alive. Being able to overcome a serious accident or a major illness is a success. There's no one definition for success. But there is one characteristic that all successful people have in common. They are not the same person they once were. Though there are obstacles in our life we must overcome, it is not impossible if we are determined. Success should not make us less humble, it should make us more appreciative. Pray daily ... be diligent in your quest to succeed ... and follow your heart.

*Sometimes in life, the fact you made an effort means more than the results of your effort. All most of us need to know is if someone cares.*

Sometimes, the results of our efforts to help others is less meaningful to them than the fact that we loved them enough to make the effort. What we give from our heart is always returned to us twofold or more. Having a servant's heart is what God wants of us. Our time is one of our most precious gifts. When we give it to someone it's added to their heart and, hopefully, overflows onto someone else in their life.

Knowing what to say or what to do is not as important as showing you cared enough to try. Our heart is both strong and fragile. It is strong in enduring the hardships of life and being faithful to those we love. But it is extremely fragile in many other ways. What hides behind all the strengths our heart shows is a tender, needy side that we rarely show. It is the place in our heart where we keep feelings like shyness, timidity, fear of rejection, loneliness, and self-worth. These emotions are in everyone's heart. The one thing that satisfies all of these emotions is the feeling of knowing someone cares. The knowledge that you matter and someone noticed you is uplifting. It is not the works we do that mean the most, but the heart behind them that make the difference. Open your heart and reach out to someone today... we all need it.

*Never stop leading. Where one person may follow you, many more may follow them, and you never know how many lives you are touching.*

One of the things that we all must realize is that no one is completely invisible. No matter how hard we try to blend in or not be noticed, we are seen every day. Whether you realize it or not, you are leading people every day with your words, behavior, or appearance. People look at other people. That's what we do, and we do it every moment we are around other people. Knowing this, we should strive to be as good an example as we can. My father, W. Howard Carpenter, gave the following advice to me when I was growing up, and it has stayed with me all these years. "For every person who sees you and knows you, there are hundreds who see you and don't know you. Their only impression is what they see at that very moment. Be your best, act you best, and treat people with respect because you never know who is watching… it could be a child." Leading is part of living every day. What you do people either follow, ignore, or adapt to themselves. We never know the amount of people we directly lead or indirectly have led through the actions of others who follow us. Take this knowledge and know you make a difference every day. You must become the best example you can be.

*The effort it takes someone to run a marathon could be the same effort it takes another to move an inch. A victory is never one definition.*

There are many victories won every day by people that none of us know. Their victories are in being able to do the things we take for granted. Taking one step, speaking one word, recognizing a loved one, or remembering who they are today...are victories of monumental proportion. The ability to do what they have done is as difficult for them as running a marathon would be for most of us. God loves every task we accomplish no matter the distance covered, the number of words we spoke, or the time it took us to accomplish it. Every victory is a blessing.

*Today, a miracle will happen in a friend's life because of something you said or did that they've never forgotten. You touch lives every day.*

Every day, we have interactions with friends, coworkers, and new people we meet. We have our usual laughs, serious discussions, and casual remarks. We do this every day and never realize that we may have said something that someone took to heart and will never forget. It is amazing what we can say without ever realizing it. Some of the greatest impact we make in life is done without us realizing it. What we say and what we do leaves an impression. How someone interprets what we say and do is also part of the impact we make. A simple pleasantry on our part may be a learning experience to someone else. A kind gesture we show someone may tell another it's OK to trust people. We touch lives every day. This is why a miracle will happen to someone today because of something they heard, saw, or experienced and they never forgot.

*One of the best assets someone can possess is empathy. If people feel you understand what they're feeling, they are strengthened.*

There is a difference between sympathy and empathy. When someone is going through a tough time and you say something like "It will be OK" or "I know how you feel," you are showing sympathy and that's good, but it's not what they may need to hear at that moment. To them, nothing will ever be OK and you really don't know how they feel because you are not them. Empathy is when you say things like, "I know you are hurting and I am so sorry" or "if there's anything I can do for you, please let me." As I have written before, when we are facing tough times, we may need to talk to someone or we may just need their silent presence. Showing empathy is when you realize what is needed. Think about what you would need from others if you were in their situation and follow your heart.

*There is nothing you cannot overcome if you understand it all doesn't have to be done today. Small steps lead to great accomplishments.*

Part of the problem all of us have at times is thinking that everything has to be done today. We get caught up in this thought pattern, and it causes us to worry more about getting something done than getting it done correctly. Some people respond well under pressure, most of us don't. Unless it is something we have put off too long and are now forced to complete quickly, taking your time and doing it in small steps usually produces a better result. But human nature will always be to get it done and out of the way. Sometimes, that's where problems begin.

*The amount of influence you have in life is determined by how much respect others have for you. Receiving respect is a gift returned to you.*

In life, we begin by developing character, and when we display character many times people realize we have integrity. When our integrity is shown to those around us, people develop respect for us. There is no other way to earn someone's respect. Character becomes integrity and integrity breeds respect. When you are respected, it is because you have shown respect to others. No respect is earned by demanding it. It has to be given to you as a returned gift that you gave others in the past. Having respect does not mean you are the best. It means you are the most trusted and others believe in you. Once obtained, respect must be continually reinforced by continued consistent respectful behavior. As I stated in my latest book... it will be the thing that speaks for you when you are not there to speak for yourself.

*Too often, we center on whether we succeeded at what we set out to do and forget all we accomplished along the way. Be proud of yourself.*

Where we start and where we end up in life requires a lot of sacrifices and a tremendous amount of dedication. We give ourselves goals in life, and we strive to accomplish them. Sometimes, we don't quite make our goal, and we feel we did not succeed. The real truth is we succeeded many times on the way to where we ended up, even if it was short of where we were headed. We should be proud of anything we decide to attempt... proud of our quest along the way... and realize we did accomplish a lot from where we started. Success is not always achieving a goal, but also looking back on how many steps we have come from where we started. Be proud of the venture, and be proud of yourself. You accomplished more than you think.

# *The simplest steps lead to the greatest accomplishments when they are followed repeatedly. Don't overthink what has already been proven.*

There are many things in life today that people think need to be changed. It is almost like they feel if it was done in the past, we must not do it that way now. Raising kids, teaching in school, mathematics, and a whole litany of other proven methods are questioned and attempted to be modified. The old saying "If it ain't broke, don't fix it" never seems too important. If something works perfectly the way it's being done now, why does it make sense to change it? As the writing states, the simplest steps lead to the greatest accomplishments when they are followed repeatedly. Don't overthink what has already been proven. A new way is not always the best way when the old way worked time after time after time. The best example of changing something that has worked for hundreds of years is the new Common Core way of teaching math. It's the most ridiculous way of doing math I have ever heard. It adds *numerous* steps arriving at an answer to the simplest math question. The biggest problem with following the Common Core way of math is not the additional steps, but the difficulty in applying the method in real life. For example, if your boss asked you how much would fifteen tablets of paper cost at $2.50 per tablet, he/she would expect you to give them answer quickly, not say, "Let me get a piece of paper and a pencil and I'll let you know after I do the twenty steps to arrive at the answer." The old way that has been proven to work should never be questioned. New is not always better.

*What we did in life is what most people will remember. But our greatest accomplishment may not have been what we did, but what we overcame.*

It is rare that someone who has become successful did so with no challenges in life. I imagine some people inherit greatness, but most of the time you have to work for it. Before I go any further, let me give you my definition of a successful person. A successful person is someone who has accomplished their maximum potential, has overcome obstacles in their life, and/or left an impression on others through their character and integrity. It is a person who will be remembered as much for what they did for others as what they accomplished in life. Success is as much about what you overcame as what you accomplished.

There is nothing in your life that will make a bigger impression on you than adversity. It will teach you the meaning of struggle, fear, hard work, overcoming obstacles, and finally, the thrill of succeeding. Those who have had to endure adversity appreciate more what they have. We all have struggled, but some have risen from a depth that few of us understand. Learn to appreciate everyone ... you never know where they came from to be where they are now.

*The best explanation for who you are is not the words you say, but the behavior you display. What people see means more than what they hear.*

Everything we do in life is judged first by what people see. Whether it's your appearance, your performance, your demeanor, or your attitude what people see is the first impression they have. You can try to explain away all of the above, but fairly or unfairly, the behavior you display is everything. Your behavior is more than doing a few things right. It's doing the right things consistently. People who are admired build themselves from the inside out. If your heart is about others and you have pride in yourself, the positive person you display will be what people will remember.

*Life is sometimes like walking on the beach. We look for a path to follow, but the footprints go in every direction. Don't follow ... lead.*

We have all been to a beach and seen the hundreds of footprints depressed in the sand. They go in every possible direction. Some overlap others, and some seem to go in a straight ordered path. Some of the footprints are nearer to the water than others, and some are there for only as long as it takes the waves to come to shore and wash them away. Life is sometimes like walking on the beach. We see a path that we wonder if we should follow. As we start to place our feet in the footprints, we see other footprints crossing over the ones we follow or walking away from where we are headed. We begin to question if we are going in the right direction, and we become confused and are afraid to move, so we just stop and go nowhere. This is when we realize we can no longer look for a path to follow. We need to create our own path for others to follow. Don't be afraid to lead. Don't be afraid to fail. Don't be afraid of criticism from others. Make your own path and stay on it. You are a leader at heart, and you must believe you will succeed.

A few years ago, I wrote something titled "Is It Only a Wave?" This is a little different perspective of the footprints on the beach. I hope you enjoy it.

# Is It Only a Wave?

I walked along the beach today
and saw more than I'd seen before.
In the footprints that preceded me
I wondered what prayers they must hold.
Maybe a lonely soul looking for answers,
A young couple sharing plans for their future,
or,
possibly an older couple,
walking hand in hand,
their love still strong
after all these years.
As I thought what dreams
must be in those footprints,
I began to see what I had never seen before.
I saw God's hand in the waves
that washed over those footprints.
One by one
every wave,
like God's hand,
took from the beach
all the footprints it could reach
and the prayers buried within them.
With just the wave of God's hand
the sand was wiped clean
and those prayers were now with Him.
Can you see what I saw?
They may just be waves,
but, just to be sure,
I walk closer to the water now.

*The words "I believe in you" are some of the most powerful words spoken. They say "I love you" in a way that motivates someone to succeed.*

A few months ago, I wrote something similar to this one, and in that writing I stated that next to saying "I love you," saying "I believe in you" is one of the best things you can say to someone. Within the words "I believe in you," you are telling someone that the course they are following, the direction they are headed, and the strength to do it are the things you see in them. When people feel they are supported and believed in, they are empowered. When someone feels their hard work is recognized and appreciated, they want to continue what they are doing. These words may be what they need to hear to give them a final push to overcome something. Believing is a synonym for such words as faith, love, and hope. With these three words in anyone's life, they are sure to feel stronger and more motivated.

*The person who is hurt most by lack of forgiveness is the one carrying the grudge. It takes up space in their heart meant for happiness.*

When something happens to us that hurts our feelings or makes us mad, our first—we feel—justifiable reaction is to hold a grudge. Forgiveness is the furthermost thing from our mind and certainly our heart. We have been scorned, and we will not tolerate it! Sound familiar? This has happened to me far more than I choose to admit. When we are hurt, our pride becomes a huge part of our emotions. We feel we must defend ourselves and harbor ill feelings against a person because we don't want them to think we will accept being treated that way. This happened to me over thirty-two years ago, and I just recently forgave a person that I hated (yes, it was hate, sorry). When I did it ... it was liberating. I felt a heaviness lift from my heart and mind. That hate no longer dominated my thoughts and my emotions. I no longer gave that person control over me and my life. We all want to be happy, and our happiness is dependent on us making ourselves happy, not looking for someone else to give us happiness. If you are holding a grudge, let it go. It is only taking up space in your heart that should be reserved for happiness.

*Wisdom is not learned from a book. It comes from remembering the mistakes you made in life and not wanting others to make the same ones.*

Many years ago, my father once said, "You can't put a forty-year-old head on a sixteen-year-old body. That's why we make so many mistakes as we are growing up." I never knew how true that was until I became a forty-six-year-old man that had a sixteen-year-old son. But more importantly, I remember the mistakes I made. I remember those moments when I would wonder, what was I thinking? Living through the mistakes in our life are what teaches us what not to do in the future. They are what creates more than knowledge, they create wisdom. The difference between knowledge and wisdom is if you are knowledgeable you realize the mistake you made. If you are wise, you realize why you made the mistake and you remember next time not to repeat it. Also what comes with wisdom is being able to apply your mistakes to life lessons. Wisdom acquired through experience gives you the ability to see behavior that will lead to mistakes that cause problems in the future. You also realize what the lasting effects will be of those mistakes. You will want to explain this to those getting ready to make those mistakes. But they will not listen, just as you did not listen and you will discover, "You can't put a forty-year-old head on a sixteen-year-old body."

*The dreams we have for our life are more than wishes in our mind. They are paths we follow to greater successes ahead. Believe in your dreams.*

Believe in your dreams... they are the glimpses of what your heart knows you can accomplish. I have written this hundreds of times in books I have sold. There has never been anything invented that wasn't first dreamed of by someone. Dreaming of what you want to do, want to invent, or want to improve has been the path anyone who accomplished anything followed. God gave us a mind to allow us to improve our world. He gave us the ability to think deeply and broadly. What may seem impossible today could be tomorrow's newest invention. A small child tinkering with a computer, putting together blocks, or drawing shapes on paper could be tomorrow's greatest inventor. Believing in your dreams are what we should always do. The key is to follow through with the dream and make it a reality.

*The best person to be a miracle, share a blessing, or make a difference in someone's life is you. Don't rely on others to do what you can do.*

As we go through life, we see and hear so many things that make us think we should do something about it, but we don't. This does not make us a bad person, but often we don't do anything because we feel we lack the skills to really help. We feel if we do step forward and try to help, we will then be committed to continue, and we don't feel we could do that. The truth is miracles happen through the simplest gestures. Blessings are given by just caring. Making a difference begins when we act on our emotions instead of being held back by our fears. There is no reason to think that because you helped someone you are now committed to continue doing so. Gestures of love can be done one time, and they still make a difference. You are the best person to do what needs to be done, because you have a heart that cares, and that's all it takes to change a life.

*Sometimes in life we are afraid to take a step due to uncertainty. Nothing has ever been accomplished without some degree of uncertainty.*

Building the confidence needed to attempt something is sometimes hard to do. We let our fears of failure hold us back. We let our pride hold us back because we don't want others to see us fail. We must remember, nothing has ever been accomplished without some degree of uncertainty. Someone had to take a chance and accept the failures that often accompany first-time attempts. It has been widely written that Thomas Edison failed two thousand times before he finally succeeded in inventing the first light bulb. Where would we be today if he had stopped trying and no one else tried because of all his failures? Making mistakes and not succeeding at what we do is normal. The simplest tasks take many attempts to perfect. If you fail, it only means you found another way not to do something, and you now know what won't work. Failing at something is as productive as succeeding. Both have accomplished something, and you learned something from both exercises. Believe in yourself and don't stop trying. The key is to not repeat the same mistakes and expect different results. You can do most things if you believe in what you're doing.

*The strength within your heart is greater than the weaknesses in your life. Whatever your mind lacks in resistance, your heart can overcome.*

This is one of my most favorite things I have ever written. Your heart is the strongest thing in your life. It can overcome anything your mind thinks you need to do. Your mind can rationalize any type of behavior. It can give you all sort of reasons why you should do or not do something. But your heart will tell you differently, and if you follow it, you will soon realize you were about to make a mistake. The problem is the weaknesses in our life originate in our mind and are reinforced each time we give into them. This is how addictions begin and also why they are so hard to break. Your mind speaks to you constantly. It tells you things like "one more time and not again" and "you can quit anytime you want." The problem is your mind is easily convinced to continue the bad behavior. The only way to break the cycle is to become convinced in your heart that you need to and you fight your mind every day for control of your life. Your faith is a good foundation to rely on to help you overcome your minds weaknesses. You must believe: whatever your mind lacks in resistance, your heart can overcome.

*A smile can hide a broken heart crying silently. If people smile and look away when asked how they are, there may be tears on their heart.*

Every day we see people smiling and assume they are happy. They seem to smile easily and are always friendly. The real truth is that some people are hiding a lot of sadness. Smiles are not always smiles of happiness. The way to know if some people are hiding some pain in their life is when they smile at you and then look away. This is because they may look happy, but they are not. Many people shed tears openly when they are sad. But there are tears that hide behind some smiles. These tears are not shed from their eyes, but shed from their heart. These are the tears we cannot see and the tears that change people's life.

I wrote something titled "Inside a Tear" that will explain more precisely what I mean.

# Inside a Tear

If you could look inside a tear
you would see what's inside a person's heart.
You would see happiness and joy
or sadness and pain.
Inside a tear
are the walls we hide behind.
We cry when we need to
and we cry when we have to.
Inside a tear you will find
the root of a person's soul.
Their loves, their hates and their deepest fears
will slide slowly down their cheek
and eventually fall to the ground,
or be wiped away
along with the reason for their tears.
God allows us to embrace our tears.
Because of this,
He gives us moments in our life
where our tears will be our only avenue
to cleanse our soul once more.

# LOVE

*"Hatred stirs up strife, but love covers all offenses"*

*—Proverbs 10:12 NRSV*

*Our arms reach only so far, but our heart has no limit. Love is a bridge across oceans or a single step toward someone needing to be loved.*

The limitations of our heart cannot be measured. Its capacity is bottomless and bound only by our own prejudices and judgments. Our ability to love someone miles away, as much as we love someone standing next to us, is amazing. Love is our bridge across physical miles and our bridge to the past we will never forget. Though our arms can reach only so far, our heart has the ability to reach as far as necessary to let someone know they're loved.

*Acts of love start in your heart, and they build slowly until your heart can no longer hold them and the excitement to do them becomes too much.*

The ability to love someone has to be one of God's greatest blessings to us. To possess the emotions to express our love to someone is what makes life worth living. Love is far more of a mental thing than a physical thing. Because of this, we constantly search for that next act of love we can show. Creating acts of love begins when you listen to and watch someone you love. You notice them looking intently at something, or you hear them casually say they like something, and soon you know what your next act of love will be. Of course, bear in mind, you may be getting set up, but you don't care. The plan to perform this act of love is formulated, and you make the mistake of planning it in the future. This is a mistake because when it comes to expressing our love to someone, we have no patience. The act of love begins to build slowly in your heart until it literally possesses your every thought and the excitement to do it becomes too much. Your plan is falling apart and suddenly it's over. She/he loves what you did and you feel relieved it's over. Unfortunately, acts of love are addictive, and you know soon this is all going to happen again.

*Touching someone without touching them*
*requires you move them emotionally.*
*The tenderest touch has always been*
*one heart embracing another.*

The power of touch is indescribable when it is wanted or needed. There is equal power in the touch of words or loving gestures that move our emotions. Touching someone without ever touching them requires that you move their emotions and embrace their heart. A friend in need, a loved one going through heartache, or a neighbor dealing with a tragedy all need the healing power of touch. Never let anyone that you can console hurt. Never allow a need to go unfulfilled if it's within your means to help. And be that person who reaches out to others before they drift beyond your reach.

*We must learn to recognize God's hands*
*of love when they are extended to us.*
*They may not hold what we want,*
*but they possess what we need.*

As we go through life, we encounter moments when we struggle or are at a loss what to do. We create some of our own problems, but we also have some thrust upon us. Most of the time, we can handle these moments ourselves, but there are times when what we do doesn't work and we need help. We need to understand that what we go through, someone we know may have also gone through it, and their advice would help. For most of us, we are quick to help others anytime they need it, but we are slow to accept help when offered. God puts people in our life for a reason. Some people are in our life because of their love for us. Others are there because they have the capacity to focus on us and help us through moments of weakness. Whatever the reason, they are the hands of God being extended to you. Don't let pride or guilt get in the way of embracing God's hands of love. They are strong, certain in their purpose, and never judgmental. God loves you, and His angels are always surrounding you.

*Our greatest love for someone may
not be the most noticeable. Love is
not always what we do, but what we
choose not to do because of them.*

Love is more than the things we do for each other. It is also loving someone enough not to do some things. When we love someone, our mind-set becomes more about them and less about ourselves. All of our decisions become how they will affect those we love. There are things we may want to do, but we realize doing them would either take away time or money from those we love. Love is multifaceted, and therefore, it is as much about what we don't do, as what we do.

*Our body may grow old, but our heart
will never age as long as there is love in
our life. Love keeps our heart young.*

We can do little about our body aging. We can work out, eat healthily, and try to keep a positive attitude, but we're going to age. The thing that can help us age gracefully is to have love in our life. Love keeps our heart young. When you're in love, the thoughts in your heart never age. No matter how old you get, love still has the same wonderful effect on your life. Keep love in your heart and you'll never feel old.

*Every person you've ever loved still lives somewhere in your heart. They may not be with you, but they're never farther than a memory away.*

One of our greatest gifts from God is our ability to love. Through love, we experience every other emotion. Our ability to love one another changes our life more than anything else and, sometimes, causes us deep pain. The pain associated with love runs deeper than any other wound we endure. But the wonderful thing about love is it becomes our reason to live, our reason to change, and our most important motivation. Those we love in our life stay with us forever. Death cannot take them away from us. It cannot take away our memories. It only makes them more precious. Take a moment and think about all the people you have loved in your life. They're still there... waiting to be smiled at once again.

*Family is not about what brings us together, but what holds us together. Love is the mortar that binds together those we call family.*

Family is very important, even if you are not close to them. Having people that you can call family goes beyond our relatives. A family is more than bloodlines and marriage. It's also those who love you no matter what, defend you if needed, and straighten you out when necessary. Family is held together by love, and that love is essential to the strength of the family. Unfortunately, the love we share is not always accepted. The love we give to those we care for is not always returned equally. We can only send out our love and hope it is embraced. Family is more than blood—it is people in our life that changed us and we will never forget. Never give up on love or those you love. Without it... loss of hope is not far behind.

*In life, what we breathe in, we also
exhale. If we breathe in love around
us, we will exhale love to others.
Take a deep breath, then share.*

Every day we make choices that tell others who we are. Some of the choices we make are who and what we are going to surround ourselves with. The old saying "You are judged by the company you keep" is true in many ways. No matter how strong we are, if we surround ourselves with those things that we know are our temptations, we make it harder to resist the temptations. I was giving a talk recently, and when I referred to the power of temptation one of the comments I made about avoiding temptation was "An alcoholic shouldn't go into a package store to buy a pack of gum." The same goes for how we keep an attitude of grace. If you surround yourself with people who have no Christian values, you may become weak and begin to lose yours. It takes a strong person to resist the easier ways to live in this world. Always put yourself in a place that allows you to breathe in the love this world has to offer. When you do, you will begin to exhale that love and begin to change your life. It's never too late to begin breathing in what you know you need in life. Love can cure anything, including yourself. Go ahead and take a deep breath, then share it with someone you love.

*There's never a moment when saying*
*I love you is unnecessary. Every*
*time you do, you leave a memory on*
*someone's heart they will feel later.*

Saying I love you is sometimes something people forget to say, but truly feel in their heart. I know loving someone is more than these words. It's about what you do and how you show it that is even more important. But letting people you love verbally hear you say the words leaves an impression on their heart. We all love to be encouraged, complimented, and made to feel special. When you say I love you, it tells that person what's in your heart is important enough to say to you. Have a blessed day.

*Some think loving others has become more difficult. If so, it's because we have drifted away from the teachings of why we should love others.*

Loving others has always been something we have been taught. From the time we were a child our parents always taught us to be kind, considerate, respectful, and friendly. In today's world, those traits should still exist, but some have trouble doing them. We are bombarded twenty-four hours a day, seven days a week with the evils of this world, the corruption of our society, and the constant message that you are not safe and you should trust no one. If all you were exposed to was hate, then being afraid would be expected. If this is all you watched or heard, why would you ever love anyone you didn't already know? Sadly, our country has slowly moved away from the church as a guide for our life. The things our parents taught us to do are questioned by society. If you listen to the media, they will tell you that the Golden Rule has been rewritten to say, "Do unto others before they do unto you." This must change. We must find a way to coexist with each other. Until we learn to trust first and judge later if we were wrong, we will never change. It can start with me, and it can continue with you. Let's fall back on "the old ways" of treating each other. Let's extend our hand instead of raising our fist. Let's speak about building harmony, addressing the problems intelligently, and trust we all are working toward the same goal. Loving one another can still happen if we learn to look at others as we would like for them to look at us. Sound familiar? Have a blessed day.

*Begin every day thinking about someone you love. It resets your heart to face all the challenges the rest of the day.*

Every day, we know we are going to face challenges. Beginning our day with thoughts about someone we love gives us a positive outlook and something to refer back to when things get tough. Every day, we encounter many things that will either challenge us, surprise us, confuse us, or make us shake our head in wonder. Unless we maintain a positive attitude, what we encounter could affect the way we treat others or feel about ourselves. Thinking of someone you love lets you know you are never truly alone in anything you deal with.

*Some people accomplish great things, and others are great at life. If you genuinely love others and are forgiving, this will be your greatness.*

Throughout our life, we witness many people accomplishing great things. We admire those accomplishments and seem to set them apart from the rest of us. They deserve that recognition due to their sacrifices and determination in obtaining that great accomplishment. But the definition of greatness has never been just a single definition. Greatness is displayed every day by many people. Greatness is doing something that makes others better. It is loving others in a way that gives them confidence in themselves. It is understanding that everyone makes mistakes. It is living your life in a way that others want to know how you do it. It is being that example that people tell others about. Greatness is accomplishing something, but it is not always just a personal accomplishment. It is seeing the accomplishments of others because of your love and support. Everyone is great ... just at different things that are less noticeable.

*In life, we only have so much time to share our love with others. Don't subtract from it by being mad, hurtful, or solitary most of the time.*

Loving others is one of the greatest pleasures we have in life. It costs nothing to do, but it can mean everything to someone else. The time we spend loving others is never wasted time. It is time we seem to add to our life because it enriches our heart. Sadly, though, there are times when we are going to get upset, mad, or hurt. These will be the times when showing our love will be the most difficult. The problem is when we get upset, mad, or hurt we have a tendency to fall back on less-loving emotions like pride, revenge, and manipulation. We feel we have to defend ourselves, and we say things we should not say. We begin to ignore the person we profess to love so much. Even if we feel remorseful for what we do and say, it makes no difference. You can't reel back in words you have already cast. We only have so much time in life to love one another. If you get your feelings hurt, go to that person and get it behind you. Loving is so much more fun than creating a void between you and someone you love just to prove a point. Loving others adds to your life…anything that keeps you from doing that only subtracts from it.

*The love we draw from that allows us to show affection should be the same love we draw from to show forgiveness. There is no difference.*

When we fall in love with someone, our life changes in so many ways. Our thoughts of how to show them our love and the hopes of a long future together brings us joy. We are completely engulfed in loving them and cherish every moment together. But the inevitable will one day happen. They will do something that will make us mad or even break our heart. Suddenly, our thoughts are no longer how to make them happy, but how to love them again. If the love you felt at the beginning was based on them behaving all the time, you may be in a bad situation. There is an old saying that has always been true. "We like someone because … we love someone although." Of course, there are some offenses that are unforgivable. These are not the ones I mean. Love is a rough road we travel that has many bumps along the way. Forgive what is forgivable because the love that made you want them so long ago is the same love that can heal your heart today.

*"I love you" is beautiful; "I'm proud of you" is uplifting; But when you say, "I believe in you," that says both and that can change their life.*

Being told you are loved by someone makes your heart feel blessed. Being told someone is proud of you gives you strength and purpose. But being told someone believes in you encompasses everything about you. It says they not only love and are proud of you, it says they understand you as a person. Your values and beliefs are something they support. It says they trust you and entrust in you their confidence. When someone believes in you, they remove any judgments concerning decisions you may make. Having trust in someone and having the confidence in them is high praise. It's possible to love someone and not have confidence in them. You can be proud of someone and not really be that close to them. But to say you believe in someone puts you side by side with them. Next to being loved ... being believed in is a close second.

*The words "I believe in you" are some of the most powerful words spoken. They say I love you in a way that motivates someone to succeed.*

A few months ago, I wrote something similar to this one and in that writing I stated that next to saying "I love you," saying "I believe in you" is one of the best things you can say to someone. Within the words "I believe in you," you are telling someone the course they are following, the direction they are headed, and that the strength to do it is something you see in them. When people feel they are supported and believed in, they are empowered. When someone feels their hard work is recognized and appreciated, they want to continue what they're doing. These words may be what they need to hear to give them a final push to overcome something. Believing is a synonym for such words as faith, love, and hope. With these three words in anyone's life, they are sure to feel stronger and more motivated.

*The touch of your hand will be felt for a moment, but the touch of your words can last forever. Make them full of love and worth remembering.*

How many times has this happened in our life? Words spoken both in harshness and in love linger in our heart and mind forever. I can remember the words special people in my life said to me over forty years ago. I cherish every word to this day. When we reach out and take someone's hand, either to hold them or shake their hand, the touch lingers for a few minutes, but the words we say after that could be what they remember. Words that touch our heart sometimes never go away. This is good when they were words of love and encouragement. Sadly, words of hate and words meant to hurt are not forgotten either. Sometimes, we don't realize that our words hurt someone. This is why we should think before we speak. Lastly, never forget, love is not conveyed in a loud voice, and starting a sentence with "You know I love you" doesn't mean you can say whatever you want after that.

*Next to saying you love someone, saying you believe in them means almost as much. We are all unsure at times; hearing this gives us strength.*

Love in our life is a powerful emotion. It can take a heart that is completely broken and mend it over time. It can hold together two people that endure hardship and heartache. Without love in your life, you live only on the surface and never deeply. A very important part of love is believing. Believing in something or someone is more than a part of love. It is the foundation for love, along with respect. Believing in someone is as important to a relationship as loyalty and forgiveness. Believing in someone tells them you are sure of their strength and that you are certain of their ability to do whatever they choose to do. The great thing about believing in people is you don't have to love them to tell them you believe in them. But I think if you truly believe in someone you do actually love him or her. What motivates us is what touches our heart. What makes us strive to move ahead is what we feel about ourselves and what we can accomplish. Having someone tell you they believe in you is almost like having them with you. In many ways, they are with you. They are in your mind and heart, reminding you that you are not alone as you try every day to succeed.

Believing in something or someone is empowering. When you tell someone you believe in him or her, you are now part of that person's life. You have a responsibility to mentor people, to encourage them, and to emotionally support them. Love is believing and believing is loving. This is what God is all about. He loves us and believes in us. When we believe in Him, we are showing Him we love him.

## *Most of the guilt we carry around with us has been forgiven or forgotten by those who love us. The only one left to forgive us ... is us.*

Our greatest gesture of love will always be forgiveness, especially when we apply it to ourselves. Forgiving is not forgetting. It's knowing mistakes are less important than loving. What our memory keeps reminding us of has probably been forgotten about by all around us. The reason it may not have been is because of our behavior or we have made the mistake repeatedly. You must allow your mistakes to live in your past. You must use them and learn from, not recall them every moment of the day. By not letting them go, you only make your life much harder than it needs to be, or it hinders your ability to move onto bigger successes.

Guilt is a terrible thing in our life, and we often suffer with feelings of guilt. The problem is that guilt tells us we could have done more, said more, or been more aware. The problem with believing this is that guilt lies all the time. Don't let it stop your healing. You must overcome the embarrassment of guilt. You have to accept your past mistakes and don't repeat them. People quickly forget your mistakes when you own up to them, accept the consequences of the mistakes, and make an effort to not repeat them. People want to be forgiving. Those who hold grudges or try to hold you back by reminding you of the mistakes are not your friends. A friend would forgive another friend. If someone who claims to be your friend continually uses your guilt to get you to do things, then you can rest assured, they need to be removed from your life. God loves you and He forgives and forgets.

*Some memories are followed by the rest of the story ... what happened next? This is the part that makes us smile or makes our heart ache.*

We all have memories that linger with us. Some make us happy and we smile. Others make us happy, but then we realize what happened after this memory. Having memories gives us a bridge back to the past and those we loved so dearly. Times gone by are meant to either teach us, lead us, or give us strength. Sometimes, our memories are our "time out" from a reality not so pleasant.

Memories are God's gift to us for a life lived. If we didn't have memories, we would not know a happiness that once was or a moment in our life we don't want to repeat. Memories are our stepping stones back to someone we once loved but have lost. They are our moments of comfort and reflection that bring back to life a time we will never forget. Sadly, there are many memories we possess that make us smile, but then we remember something that happened afterward. To have the wonderful memories we possess, we must understand they are not all going to be a happy one. Even these memories we should treasure because they are the ones that taught us something that helped us through life or changed our life forever. Be happy with your life. No one else has the same memories you do. Have a wonderful day and make some new memories today you can smile about tomorrow.

*Love can only be as strong as those
who possess it, as tender as the
feelings they share, and as true as the
openness and trust between them.*

One of the main premises of the Bible, and something Jesus taught us to do, was love one another. We are meant to have love in our life. We are meant to find love in our life. It was because of love that Christ died on the cross. Loving one another and having only one God in our life was what we are taught to do as Christians.

Throughout our life, we have many loves. When you find someone special that you know is going to be the love of your life, you must develop a special bond with them. The bond is not only something physical, but also something that will connect you for a lifetime. When you find that bond, you become stronger. You become as one, and together your love will be as strong as you both are, as tender as the feelings between you and as true as the openness and trust you both display to each other. Love is more than a heart thing. It is a mind, body, and soul thing also. What you pledge to each other is a sacred oath. Your mind, your heart, and your soul are centered entirely on each other. If that is your mind-set, and you do not deviate from that, your love will last. Every decision you make has an effect on those you love. Make your decisions to be the best you can be for them. If they do the same, nothing will ever pull you apart.

*Death may take those we love from our sight, but it cannot take them from our heart. What our eyes no longer see, our heart never forgets.*

The death of someone we love is never easy. Because of the memories they leave behind, what our eyes may no longer see, our heart will never forget. Memories of those we loved are captured moments that abide in our heart until we need them to teach us, guide us, or remind us that they never really left us. The amount of love our heart possesses is endless. Our opportunities to show it are not. Tomorrow is never the best day to say I love you.

We have so many people in our life that we love. With everything we have to focus on daily, we sometimes don't let them know how much they mean to us. Life is so unpredictable, and the opportunities we have to say I love you seem endless, but they aren't. Our greatest fear is losing someone and realizing we should have let them know how much we loved them. We cannot dwell on what we should have done; we can only realize what we need to do. Look for your opportunities, and let someone know they are loved.

*Memories are the wealth we inherit when someone we love passes away. No one who left a memory in your heart is ever forgotten.*

There are many things that happen to us throughout our life. Some are memorable, and others are like light breezes that blow past us. When we meet someone and they leave a smile in our life, they also leave fingerprints on our heart. Sometimes, we realize those fingerprints are there, but often they don't appear until a moment when we suddenly recall something they said or did. These are inheritances we receive after they are gone. Through our memories, no one who ever touched our heart and left a fingerprint will ever be forgotten. Love has a way of imprinting people on our heart, as well as their fingerprints. Love seems to make room for people we will never forget. We may meet thousands of people in our lifetime, but only a few will be with us throughout our life. Why certain people seem to stay with us where others do not is unexplained. It may be their personality, their love for us, or their impact on our life. Whatever it is, we are blessed to have known them.

*Sometimes, when people are hurting they don't need words. They need the sound of silence that embraces their broken heart and says I love you.*

Sometimes when we are emotionally hurt, our brain wants to defend our heart. It does this by rejecting any comments of comfort. When people's hearts hurt, they pull inside themselves and don't want to think. Saying something to them makes them think, and they don't want to do that. Your comforting silence is what they need at that moment. You can talk later, once they have begun to accept the loss.

We all grieve differently. Some do so openly and are willing to accept comforting words and support. Others grieve quietly and privately process what has happened and allow themselves to slowly accept the loss. Eventually, these people open up and seek solace from friends and family. Knowing when to speak and when to be silently present is difficult. It's always best to say as little as possible and allow the grieving person to talk to you and lead you to what they need. Loving someone at their time of loss can mean doing or not doing anything. We all gain strength through support. We don't gain strength through being told everything will be all right. People are changed after the death of someone they loved. You have to be willing to accept that change. Silence can be the greatest support in the world. Let the grieving person do the talking.

# *It's more important you're everything to someone, rather than trying to be something to everyone. Those you love deserve your focus on them.*

There are many things in our life that we want to accomplish. There are many things that seem to take up our time. If you have a servant's heart, you want to help others when you can. This is a good thing if you are able to know when enough is enough and you no longer take time away from your family. We all want to be recognized for loving others. We want to give of ourselves to help others. There is a limit, though, to how much time we should give to others. Our family loves us and they want to see us. If we overschedule ourselves and our family has to be without us, we are not being all we can be for them. It is more important you're everything to someone, rather than trying to be something to everyone. When we give, we do so with our family in mind. We have to know where we belong at all times. Where we belong must always be with those we love unless they are also a part of what we are doing. Loving others is what we are taught to do. But family must come first, and our benevolence cannot negatively affect them, no matter who we are benefiting.

*True wealth is not how much you have in investments, but how much you've invested in others. Love is an appreciating asset that grows daily.*

Wealth has always been a measurement of success. People admire those that are wealthy and share their wealth. Making good investments is the key to early retirement, a secure future, and being able to help others. Investing wisely is difficult, and those who are successful at it reap the rewards of their success. There is only one investment that is guaranteed to appreciate in value. It is the only investment you will make that has gains every day. That is the investment you make in others with your time and your knowledge. By sharing with others what you know, what you understand, and what you have learned, you are making an investment in their future and in gains for yourself. These type of investments appreciate daily and are appreciated by those you invest in. Making an investment in your family, your friends, and those you love will always show gains and very few losses. Loving others enough to give them your time and commitment makes you richer every day. You may not be able to count the wealth in dollars, but you will be able to see the wealth you created in those around you. Love is never a bad investment. It has always been the investment that paid the greatest returns.

*Mending a broken heart is like putting together a jigsaw puzzle. You find a piece of your heart you recognize, and you build slowly around it.*

If you have ever had your heart broken, you know what this piece of writing is saying. We have all been through a broken relationship or had a friend turn on us, and it breaks our heart. It is difficult to know what to do or what to say. Sometimes, the heart that is broken is not ours, but a close friend's. When a friend's heart is broken, you may not know what to say or what to do, but that is OK because they may not be looking for an answer. When someone's heart is broken the pain goes farther than the physical hurt. It devastates them mentally and emotionally. When this happens, all we can do is accept the loss, look within ourselves, and find a piece of our heart we recognize and start building slowly around it until we are back together. The piece you search for to start building is the one that possesses your greatest strength (resilience, faith or self-esteem). You then start building around it with other pieces like memories or favorite places you want to go. The most important thing is that you find pieces that have not been shared with the one who broke your heart. You can only mend your heart if you throw away those pieces and start putting your heart back together with new memories. Healing your heart is difficult until you realize it's OK to be OK. It's OK to smile, it's OK to be you. Accepting the loss of someone is not forgetting. Besides, the best way to respond to someone who broke your heart is to be OK. If they see you are OK, they may feel they never really mattered anyway.

# *The amount of love our heart can hold is not measured by height or width, but by the depth of our love for those we treasure.*

To love someone and be loved by someone is the greatest feeling in the world. To know you are special enough to someone that they center all their attention on you is amazing. How much we are able to love each other cannot be measured by its height or width, but only by its depth.

There are many types of love. The love we have for our parents is different than the love we have for our spouse or girlfriend/boyfriend. The love we have for our siblings is different than the love we have for our friends. And the love we have for our children/grandchildren is different than the love we have for our spouse. All of these loves can run very deeply. So deeply you would give your life to save the one you love. God loves us this much, and His Son showed us the depth of true love when He sacrificed himself on the cross. But it is not necessary to die for someone to show them the depth of your love. We can do that by being supportive, consoling, protective, and understanding. We can also do it by holding them accountable for their actions, allowing them to suffer the consequences of their behavior, and by letting them make mistakes that will not harm them but teach them. There is no way to measure the depth of our love for someone, except to be strong when they are weak, be positive when they are negative, and be firm when they want you to give in. Love is the foundation we rely on every day. Be that foundation for those you love and love you.

*True friendships are not formed through shared good times. They are formed through shared adversity and a bond created through shared tears.*

Friendships are one of the most important relationships in our life. Friendship is the bond we form with someone that allows us to open our heart enough to be ourselves and make them part of our life. They are more numerous than our loves, and the bond formed between people that is not based on something physical is essential to our self-esteem. What we receive from those who have formed lasting friendships with us is vital to every emotion we will experience in life. Throughout our life, we go through many ups and downs. Anyone can enjoy the good times we have, but only a true friend endures with us the sadness and hardships of our life. Because of this, our relationship with a true friend is formed as much from the adversities we share together as the good times we live through together. You must have shared tears as much as shared laughs to form a strong bond with a friend. It's these shared tears that create the best memories why you care so much for your friend. Every emotion we have is expressed to our friends. If they can endure our roller coaster of emotions, they will be with us forever.

*A single tear sliding slowly down the cheek of someone you love can mean many things. Make sure it is flowing toward a smile you created.*

Within the relationships of our life there are tears that will fall. We will create some of those tears, but we will witness many of them that we had nothing to do with. If you love someone, it is always your place to comfort them when they are shedding a tear. It may not require that you say anything, but your presence will give them comfort. You may have to be the one that "hears all about it," and you will need to sit quietly and listen. If you don't, the next tears you see may have been created by your lack of attentiveness.

The happiest tears you will see will be the ones that flow slowly and softly toward a smile on someone's face. These are the tears of happiness and love. These tears are as much your responsibility to respond to as the one that have hurt someone. Your greatest joy will be when someone says thank you through a flood of tears. Tears are sometimes our only means of cleaning our soul or expressing just how much we love someone.

*Loving someone is a collection of moments lived, moments felt, and moments dreamed. Not all will be happy, but all will be worth every moment.*

The moments in life that teach us the most are not always our happiest. Many of our greatest lessons were learned through a flood of tears. Memories we carry with us are usually happy ones that we reflect back on with fondness. But just as important, we have memories that make us sad. At those moments in life, we are knocked back and frozen in place for a moment. We did not know which way to turn or to even move. The pain and the hurt we remember and never want to live again. These are the moments that taught us to never place ourselves in those situations again. We lived them once and choose not to live them again. These are the moments lived, moments felt, and moments dreamed that are with us every day. What we learn in life is not always from the happiest moments. What we remember most are not always our greatest times. We will, however, remember every moment of embarrassment, every taunt we received, and every heartbreak we endured. They are our memories, and they taught us so much.

*There's never a moment when saying I love you is unnecessary. Every time you do, you leave a memory on someone's heart that they will feel later.*

Saying I love you is sometimes something people forget to say, but truly feel in their heart. I know loving someone is more than these words. It's about what you do and how you show it that is even more important. But letting someone you love verbally hear you say the words leaves an impression on their heart. We all love to be encouraged, complimented, and made to feel special. When you say I love you, it tells that person what's in your heart is important enough to say to you. Have a blessed day.

*The amount of love our heart possesses is endless. Our opportunities to show it are not. Tomorrow is never the best day to say I love you.*

We have so many people in our life that we love. With everything we have to focus on daily, we sometimes don't let them know how much they mean to us. Life is so unpredictable, and the opportunities we have to say I love you may seem endless, but they aren't. Our greatest fear is losing someone and realizing we should have let them know how much we loved them. We cannot dwell on what we should have done; we can only realize what need to do. Look for your opportunities and let someone know they are loved.

*Today may be just another day, but you could be a miracle to someone and never know it. It only takes a moment of grace to change a heart.*

There are many moments in our life when we have a chance to teach, lead, or change someone. How we project what's in our heart can make a difference not only in ourselves, but also in those around us. There are countless numbers of people searching for a path to follow, a reason to live, and a joy they can hold on to. If we project the love and compassion we possess, we can be a miracle to others. God gives us the ability to change ourselves and those around us, and that is a miracle in itself.

*When your heart is filled with so much
love that it overflows into your life,
that's when you will begin making
a difference without trying.*

We have all known people who seem filled with love and enthusiasm. Their spirit and personality makes them fun to be around. They seem to never be down or upset about things. When they are confronted by something that would infuriate us, they seem to take it in stride or find a way to deal with it without getting emotional. The love in their heart has taught them that getting upset about something doesn't fix it or make it go away. It only delays their beginning to deal with it. People who make a difference in others don't realize they are doing so. They live their life treating everyone fairly and equally. They make a difference by being reliable and trusting. They do all of this not because they are trying to impress someone. They do this because they know treating people as they would want to be treated is the key to making a difference. Becoming a person whose heart is overflowing is more about what you are willing to give to others and less about what you expect to receive in return. Love is the answer to every situation. If we learn to love one another, everything else in our life will fall into place.

*The touch of your hand will be felt for a moment, but the touch of your words can last forever. Make them full of love and worth remembering.*

How many times has this happened in our life? Words spoken both in harshness and in love linger in our heart and mind forever. I can remember the words special people in my life said to me over forty years ago. I cherish every word to this day. When we reach out and take someone's hand, either to hold them or shake their hand, the touch lingers for a few minutes, but the words we say after that could be what they remember for years. Words that touch our heart sometimes never go away. This is good when they were words of love and encouragement. Sadly, words of hate and words meant to hurt are not forgotten either. Sometimes, we don't realize that our words hurt someone. This is why we should think before we speak. Lastly, never forget, love is not conveyed in a loud voice, and starting a sentence with "You know I love you" doesn't mean you can say whatever you want after that.

*Every decision you make isn't only about you. Those who love you live your decisions with you. Think before you speak and look before you act.*

There is an old saying that states, "It's easy to make decisions ... the hard part is making the right ones." This is very true throughout our life. There will, in some way, always be a chance you are taking when you make any decision. When you are single, the decisions you make affect mostly just you. But if you are married, the decisions you make affect both of you, and taking your spouse into consideration before making a decision is essential. The hardest decisions we make in life are the ones that are made after we have a family. Decisions such as where to live, changing jobs, and having another child are life-changing decisions for more than just you. They affect all the family members, and you must take them into consideration. Whether we enjoy it or not, those who love us live our decisions with us. They do so not because they want to influence us in any way, but because they love us and only want the best for us.

When you are young, you think you know everything. Well, you don't, and finding that out can be pretty painful if you are not careful. Rely on those with experience to guide you. If you do this, one day you too will be the one living the decisions along with someone whom you love. You will then know what it means to live the decisions of those you love.

*The sacrifices we make for those we love are not really sacrifices. They are opportunities we wait for to express how much we love them.*

Loving someone is worth every moment you are able to do so. Discovering what makes people happy and what makes them sad is part of the adventure. The smile on their face is more than an expression of happiness. It is a verification that you are succeeding in one of your most important endeavors in life. Making sacrifices is part of loving someone. In the beginning of a loving relationship, we make minor sacrifices like where to eat, what movie to see, or going somewhere you really don't enjoy because he/she wanted to go. As we get older, our attitude about making sacrifices is a little different because we know now it's not that necessary to always be together. Love can still be strong even if you are not together every waking moment. But there is another change you go through about sacrifices. This change is in the definition of what is a sacrifice. Once you have an established loving relationship, you no longer look at the things needed or asked for by the one you love as a sacrifice. Instead of being sacrifices, they become opportunities to show someone how much you love them. The love you have for them is no longer about making them happy, but about making them know you love them. Love is an amazing thing when it is shown without anything attached to it.

*Some memories we hold in our heart are moments to help us through sad times ahead. What we hold tightest to ... will always be the love.*

Memories are God's gift to us for loving someone. He gives us the ability to recall loving moments, times of joy and moments when we learned so much from someone. The moments in our life that become memories in our heart are not by accident. They are carefully placed there for us to use when we need to be reminded of who we are. They are there to take us back to a learning moment. And they are there to keep someone in our life long after they are gone. Holding on to the love is what holds us up when we need it. Treasure your every memory. These are the moments God chose to place in your heart because He knew you would need them someday.

*There are a lot of assumptions we have to make in this world. The fact that someone knows you love them shouldn't be one of them.*

Loving someone is what makes life living. Having someone to love and being loved gives us more than a purpose in life. It gives us security and solitude that can last our lifetime. But one of the things that happen when we have love in our life for a long time is we sometimes forget to verbally express it as often as we should. We know we love someone, and we just assume they know we love them. I am sure that is indeed true, but hearing someone say they love you lifts you up and fans the flames in our heart. Don't assume that someone knows you love them. Make sure they know you love them.

*His love isn't only in the heartbeats we hear, but in the pause between them. This is when God whispers, "Don't worry, I'm still here."*

God's love surrounds us, lays deep inside of us, and flows throughout our body. His words of love speak clearly to us every time our heart beats. Life sometimes pulls us away from God, and we feel distant from Him. No matter how far we may feel we have drifted from God, He is never more than a prayer away, and He whispers between our every heartbeat, "Don't worry, I'm still here." We serve a God of second chances. The only thing God is interested in is how you feel right now. He never quit loving you, so He never gave up on you. With God, there's no such thing as "it's too late."

*If you love someone, every day should begin and end with the words "I love you." The time in between is when you show them you love them.*

Loving someone and being loved by someone has no match in life. To know someone cares deeply for you gives you strength, confidence, and security. To love someone gives you purpose, hope, and dreams. The words "I love you" seem almost too simple when describing your actual feelings. We find many loves in life that seem to satisfy us emotionally, but there will be that one love that goes much deeper than others. It will be the one that changes your heartbeat, consumes your mind, and takes your breath away. If you have this love in your life, you are blessed. Never let it go and never take it for granted.

To God be the Glory
Great things He has Done.

# ABOUT THE AUTHOR

Randall Carpenter has been writing since he was a young teenager. He has written over 1,600 separate writings and most are on deposit in the Library of Congress. He holds a bachelor's degree from the University of Tennessee in Knoxville. He became a Stephen Minister several years ago, and his insights have helped many people better understand themselves and the world around them. He held the senior lay position in one of the largest Methodist churches in the United States for many years. His words, observations, and insights will open your heart to the love of God.

CPSIA information can be obtained
at www.ICGtesting.com
Printed in the USA
LVHW090822090721
692137LV00001B/57

9 781640 279940